WILD ANIMALS

Barbara Cork

Designed by David Bennett, Anne Sharples,
Andrzej Bielecki and Nicky Wainwright

Cover design by Josephine Thompson
Illustrated by Denise Finney, David Wright,
Dee Morgan, Judy Friedlander and Ian Jackson

Edited by Laura Howell
Consultant editor: Miranda Stevenson
Language consultant: Gillian Ghate

Contents

Looking at wild mammals

When people say "animals", they usually mean mammals. This book is all about wild mammals. Mammals are different from all the other animals in the world. They are the only animals that have fur or hair. Female mammals are the only animals that make milk to feed their young. You are a mammal.

Fallow deer feeding her fawn

A mammal keeps the inside of its body at the same temperature, even when it is hot or cold outside.

Polar bears

A mammal has a good brain. This chimp is using a rock as a tool.

Chimp

All mammals breathe, even mammals that live in water.

Whale

All mammals have some fur or hair on their body.

Porcupines have special hard hairs, called quills.

Musk oxen have lots of hair. This keeps them warm.

Elephants have only a few hairs.

Many mammals' coats have two kinds of hair. Beavers have thick, short, soft hairs under a layer of long, rough hairs. Only the long hairs get wet in water.

Bactrian camel

Some mammals, such as camels, grow two new coats every year. This camel is growing its thin summer coat. Its thick winter coat falls out so fast that the hair comes off in large chunks.

Winter coat

Summer coat

Go to www.usborne-quicklinks.com for a link to a Web site where you can find lots of useful and friendly information about mammals.

3

Legs and feet

Most mammals move around on four legs.

Ankle

Pandas walk on their whole foot.

Ankle

Foxes walk on their toes.

Ankle

Deers walk on their toe nails.

Back feet land in front of front feet.

A mountain hare's feet act like snowshoes. They are wide and flat and have lots of fur underneath. This helps the hare to walk or run over the snow without sinking in very far.

Otters use their tail to change direction.

Otters have skin between their toes. They can swim under water, using their feet like flippers.

 Go to www.usborne-quicklinks.com for a link to a Web site where you can read descriptions of the different ways that mammals move on land, and in the water and air.

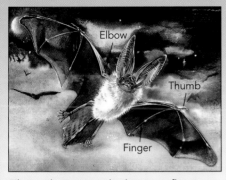

The only mammals that can fly are bats. They use their arms as wings. Thin skin is stretched over the long bones of the arm and fingers.

Kangaroo rats hop around on two legs. They use their long back feet to make huge leaps. Their tail helps them to balance.

Long, thin toes for holding onto branches

Spider monkeys use their strong tail like an extra arm or leg. They curl the tip of the tail around branches and use it to swing through the trees.

5

Teeth and feeding

Many mammals feed mainly on plants. They have a lot of grinding teeth because plants are hard to chew.

Chipmunks carry food in cheek pouches.

Hard pad is under here.

The front teeth of a chipmunk never stop growing. Its teeth do not get too long, though, as it wears them down when it feeds.

Bighorn sheep have no front teeth in their top jaw. Instead, they have a hard pad which they use to bite off the tops of plants.

Giraffes use their long tongue to eat leaves from tall trees.

Dik-diks eat leaves from bushes.

Zebras graze on grass.

Elands eat small plants.

Many different mammals can feed close together on the African grasslands. This is because they eat different kinds of plants which grow at different heights. You can see this if you look carefully at the mammals in the picture.

Go to www.usborne-quicklinks.com for a link to a Web site where you can meet some groups of mammals in a forest who all eat different things.

Fruit

Dead vole

Long, sensitive fingers help to find and catch food.

Fish

Koalas feed only on the leaves of gum trees. They will die if they cannot find the right sort of gum tree to feed on.

Raccoons feed on plants and animals. They will eat living things or dead things. A raccoon can usually find enough to eat.

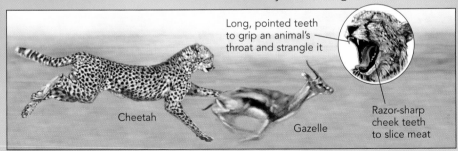

Long, pointed teeth to grip an animal's throat and strangle it

Cheetah

Gazelle

Razor-sharp cheek teeth to slice meat

Some mammals mainly eat other animals. They use lots of energy catching their food. Cheetahs may be too tired to eat for up to 15 minutes after they have killed. Meat is very nourishing, though, so they do not feed every day.

Mammals at night

More than half the mammals in the world come out at night.

Potto

Pupils open wide to let in lots of light.

Sticky pads on toes help to grip branches.

The tarsier has huge eyes and special ears that help it to see and hear well at night. It leaps through the trees, pouncing on bugs and small animals.

Many mammals have a special layer at the back of their eyes. This layer helps them to see in the dark. It makes their eyes glow if a light shines on them.

Badgers sniff the ground looking for earthworms and bugs to eat.

Badgers use their sharp sense of smell and good hearing to move around at night. They find food by sniffing the ground with their sensitive noses.

Go to www.usborne-quicklinks.com for a link to a Web site where you can find out more about bats, with pictures and activities.

Fold of skin

Many bats feed on insects that come out at night. This greater horseshoe bat eats flies and moths. It has sharp, pointed teeth to chop up its food.

Sugar gliders feed on flowers and insects at night. They stretch open folds of skin along the sides of their bodies to glide from tree to tree.

The red fox hunts at night. When it hears and smells a mouse in the grass, the fox leaps in the air like this. It will land with its front paws on the mouse.

Escaping from enemies

Sharp scales

Squirrels escape from enemies by climbing trees. They are small and light and can leap onto very thin branches. Most of their enemies cannot follow.

Pangolins have hard, overlapping scales all over their bodies. The back edge of each scale is sharp. When they roll into a tight ball, their enemies cannot hurt them.

1. This spiny anteater has sharp spines on its back. It burrows into the ground to escape from enemies.

2. It digs straight down with its long claws and sinks out of sight in about one minute.

3. When it is buried, its enemies leave it alone. The spines may cut them if they try to dig it up.

Go to **www.usborne-quicklinks.com** for a link to a Web site where you can play a game to identify how animals hide themselves.

This skunk is holding its tail up to say "Go away, or I will squirt you with my smelly liquid."

Summer

Winter

Skunks squirt a nasty liquid at enemies. The liquid comes from a gland under the tail. Most enemies leave them alone.

A mountain hare lives in places where it snows in winter. It has a brown coat in summer and a white coat in winter. This helps it to hide from enemies.

Many mammals that live in forests or jungles have striped or spotted fur. They match the shades and patterns of the trees and bushes, so they are hard for enemies to spot. Can you find eight mammals hiding in this African jungle?

Homes

Mammals build homes to keep themselves warm, dry and safe from enemies.

Rabbits live in a maze of tunnels, which they dig under the ground. This is called a warren. They run into the warren to escape from enemies.

The female harvest mouse builds a home for her young. She tears grass leaves into strips and weaves them into a round nest. It is warm and dry.

The cubs are born in the middle of winter.

The female polar bear digs a cave of ice and snow, where she can spend the winter. She does not come out until the weather gets warmer in spring.

Go to www.usborne-quicklinks.com for a link to a Web site where you can explore the homes of many types of animals, including mammals.

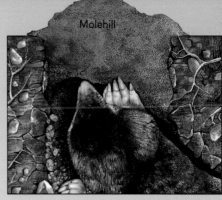

Molehill

The only home chimpanzees make is a nest where they can sleep. They bend branches over to make a bed of leaves near the top of a tree.

A mole spends most of its life inside its home. It uses its front feet like shovels to dig out tunnels in the soil. It feeds and sleeps in these tunnels.

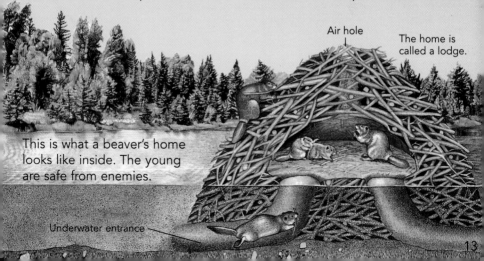

Air hole

The home is called a lodge.

This is what a beaver's home looks like inside. The young are safe from enemies.

Underwater entrance

13

Finding a mate

Female

Male

Siberian tigers

Male

Female

Female mammals often give out a special smell when they are ready to mate. A male harvest mouse sniffs a female to see if she is ready to mate.

Tigers play together before they mate. This female is asking the male to mate with her. She bites him gently and then rubs her body against his.

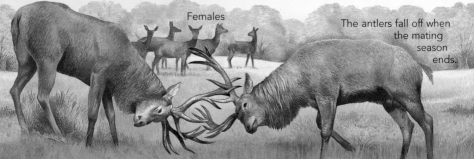

Females

The antlers fall off when the mating season ends.

Once a year, a male red deer rounds up a group of females for mating. He roars to tell other males how strong he is. If another male roars as often as he does, they fight with their antlers. The strongest male wins the females.

14

A male antelope, such as this Uganda kob, must dance in front of a female before she will mate with him.

Male   Female

Male   Female

1. The male kob holds his head up to show off the white patch under his chin. He stretches out his front legs to show off his black stripes.

2. Next, he holds his front leg out very stiff and straight. He taps the female gently with it. If she stands still, he will mate with her.

Male and female red foxes dance together before they mate. They stand on their back legs and hug each other with their front legs. They hold their mouths open and make a chattering call.

Go to www.usborne-quicklinks.com for a link to a Web site where you can see pictures showing how animals use signals to find a mate.

Having babies

After a female mammal has mated, a baby may start to grow inside her. Most baby mammals stay inside their mother until they have grown all the parts of their bodies. Then they are ready to be born.

Baby dormice are helpless when they are born. They are blind and deaf and have no hair on their bodies. They are born in a nest, warm and safe from enemies.

When zebras are born, they can see, hear and smell, and have hair all over their bodies. They can run about an hour after they are born. They stay close to other zebras. This helps to keep them safe from enemies.

Go to www.usborne-quicklinks.com for a link to a Web site where you can find friendly information and pictures of baby animals.

A few mammals are born before they grow all the parts of their bodies. Most of them finish developing in a pouch on their mother's body.

When a baby kangaroo is born, it is smaller than your little finger. It has to crawl up to its mother's pouch.

Close-up of the birth opening. The baby climbs upwards.

Looking inside the pouch

The baby holds onto a teat and sucks milk from its mother. It stays in the pouch for six months. By then, it has grown all the parts of its body.

The platypus and the spiny anteater are unusual mammals that lay eggs. A single baby grows inside each egg.

The nest is at the end of a long burrow in a river bank.

The platypus lays her eggs in a nest of leaves and grass. The eggs have a soft shell.

Growing up

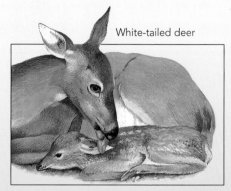

White-tailed deer

Japanese macaque

Most mammals spend a lot of time licking their young. This keeps them clean and healthy. It also forms a bond between mother and young.

A baby mammal sucks milk from glands on its mother's body. The glands produce milk as soon as a baby is born. The milk is rich in foods the baby needs.

A tigress picks up her cubs in her mouth to carry them to a safe place. The cubs do not get hurt as they keep still and their mother's jaws do not shut properly.

African elephant

Mountain goats play games with their mother and other young goats. This teaches them how to balance and climb on the steep mountain slopes.

This mother elephant is protecting her calf from an enemy. The young elephant is too small to look after itself. It stays close to its mother.

White-toothed shrews go out with their mother when they are about a week old. They hold on to each other in a long line so they do not get lost.

Go to www.usborne-quicklinks.com for a link to a Web site where you can watch videos of baby mammals in a real zoo.

Living in a group

Lions live in a group called a pride. The female lions are called lionesses. They do most of the hunting. They also feed the cubs and look after them. The male lions keep a safe area for the pride to live in.

An adult male has a thick mane. This protects his head and neck in fights. It also helps to attract a female.

Lionesses hunt in teams. They are more likely to catch large animals if they hunt together.

This is a young male. He will leave the pride when he is about three years old.

The cubs spend a lot of time playing. This helps them learn how to fight and hunt.

A lioness usually stays in the pride for life. She may feed any of the cubs. This helps them to survive.

Chimpanzees live in a group called a community. The males defend the group from enemies. They often travel and feed with other males. Females look after the young.

A chimpanzee may share its food with other members of the group. One chimp may stare at another to ask for food.

There is a top male in each group. He often charges about like this making a lot of noise. This shows the other chimps he is in charge.

Chimps crouch down like this when they meet a more important chimp. This chimp may pat them to say "I will not attack you".

Woodland chimps catch termites by poking a grass stem into their nest. Young chimps learn how to do this by watching their parents.

Chimpanzees spend a lot of time grooming their fur. This helps to keep them clean and healthy. Grooming also calms the chimps and helps them to stay good friends.

Go to www.usborne-quicklinks.com for a link to a Web site where you can find lots of fascinating facts about chimps, with a quiz to try.

Sea mammals

The only mammals that spend their whole lives in the sea are dolphins, whales and sea cows. They have few hairs and no back legs.

A dolphin's teeth are small and pointed. They are good for catching fish.

A dolphin comes to the surface to breathe air through its blowhole.

A dolphin's body is a good shape for moving fast in the water. It moves its strong tail up and down to push its body along. It uses its flippers and the fin on its back to change direction.

Mouth of a humpback whale

Bony plates

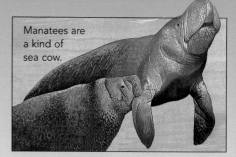

Manatees are a kind of sea cow.

Some whales have no teeth. Instead, they have rows of bony plates, which end in a thick, hairy fringe. The fringe strains tiny animals from the water.

This manatee calf is sucking milk from a teat near its mother's flipper. Manatees are born in the water and can swim as soon as they are born.

22

Seals, sea lions and walruses spend only part of their lives in the sea. They have back legs and most of them have a coat of short hair.

Long toes with skin between them

Tail

A sea lion's smooth, thin body helps it to swim fast under water. It uses its front flippers to push itself along. It uses its back flippers to change direction. It has only a short tail.

Walruses use their long teeth to dig up shellfish from the sea floor. They also use their teeth for fighting.

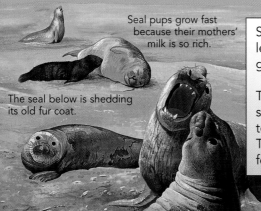

Seal pups grow fast because their mothers' milk is so rich.

The seal below is shedding its old fur coat.

Seals, sea lions and walruses leave the sea every year to mate, give birth and grow a new coat.

This is a group of elephant seals. The males fight each other to win an area of the beach. They will mate with all the females in their area.

Go to www.usborne-quicklinks.com for a link to a Web site where you can find facts and games about many kinds of sea mammals and other sea animals.

Index

First published in 2002 by Usborne Publishing Ltd., Usborne House, 83-85 Saffron Hill, London EC1N 8RT, England. www.usborne.com Copyright © 2002, 1990, 1982 Usborne Publishing Ltd.